Saving Jerry

Written by Will Jamieson

CARAMEL TREE

CHAPTER 1

The Moment of Truth

K ate was smart. Kate was really, really, smart. What made Kate special was that she wasn't smart the way that other kids at school were. Sometimes she got A's but usually she got B's or even C's. Her parents would always tell Kate that she should be doing better in school. But the truth was that they knew Kate was smart. She was always busy inventing things.

Kate had invented more things than she could count. She would spend all her time designing new inventions on her notebook, or building them in her room. Her room was

cluttered with different projects, tools, and science books.

Some of her inventions that she was most proud of were hanging on the wall. Kate had made special balloon shoes that she could use to walk on water. She had invented a rocket that she had attached to her bike so that the bike would go super-fast at the press of a button. She had even made a key that could unlock any door. She called it her *'magic key.'*

Today was extra special. Kate had been working on a new project for the past two months. When all the other kids were studying or playing outside, Kate was in her room, drawing plans and building objects. Today she was almost finished with her greatest invention ever. It had taken her hours and hours of work and now it was almost done. Kate had made a robot.

She had started building the robot as a science project for school. At first she just wanted to get a good mark, but now, all she cared about was having her own robot. Every day after school, Kate would rush home and work on her robot until her mom told her she had to go to sleep. Every morning, she would get up early and work on her robot until her mom said she had to go to school. It had become much more than a science project.

Kate sat on her desk chair looking at her robot. She had built it out of bicycle parts, a broken printer, a coffee maker, three flashlights, two old computers, a car battery, and all sorts of junk she had found in the basement. The robot had a square head with two round eyes made out of old camera lenses and a square mouth made of computer speakers. On the front of the robot was a small gauge that indicated the battery level. The robot had wheels instead of legs and metal hands with three fingers. Kate had just finished painting the robot bright red and the paint was almost dry. The robot was plugged into the wall and its battery was almost fully charged.

Kate was a little nervous. This was such a big project and if the robot didn't work, she would have wasted a lot of time. She had never spent this much time on a single project before. Kate watched the battery meter slowly move towards the green *'charged'* indicator and thought about how much fun it would be to have a robot. Not only would it be fun to play with a robot, but she could make it do her homework, clean up her room, or anything she wanted.

When the meter showed that the robot was charged, she unplugged it from the wall.

"Well, this is it!" Kate said to herself. "This is the moment of truth!" She slowly put her finger on the robot's ON/OFF switch. She took a deep breath and then turned the robot's switch to ON.

Kate stood and watched her robot to see what would happen. She was very excited. She watched the robot for a few seconds and nothing happened. Soon, seconds became minutes. Still nothing.

"Come on!" Kate said as she gave the robot's head a shake. She opened up a door on its stomach and checked some wires. *'Everything looks OK,'* she thought.

Kate was starting to get frustrated. She tried to think of what she might have done wrong. All the switches were on. The battery was fully charged. The circuit board was connected. Everything should be working.

"Ahh!" Kate screamed as she stood staring at the lifeless machine. "Stupid piece of garbage," she added as she gave the robot a kick.

It was no good. The robot was lifeless.

Kate sat down on the floor tired and frustrated. *'Maybe it's not fully charged,'* she thought. She decided to plug the robot back into the wall.

Just then, Kate's mom tapped on the door. "Bedtime, Kate," she said.

"OK, Mom," Kate replied with a sigh and got up to get ready for bed.

CHAPTER 2

The Storm

That night Kate lay in bed thinking about how much time she had spent on her robot. Not only had it all been a waste of time and parts, but now she didn't have anything to show for her science project. She would need to think of something fast because it was due in four days.

The wind was blowing hard against Kate's window and it was making a loud whistling noise outside. She could hear the tree near her window creaking back and forth and in the distance, she thought she heard thunder.

'If I take this stupid robot apart, I can use all the parts to

build something new for my science project,' she thought.

'But what could I build in such a short time?'

The wind blew louder and louder against the window, and soon it began to rain. Kate heard the thunder getting closer.

'Oh I know, what if I use the wheels from the robot to make some sort of roller shoes,' thought Kate. *'I can take out its motor and use that for...'*

KABOOM! Thunder clapped loudly and Kate saw the flicker of lightning flash across her room. The rain poured down violently against her window.

"That's getting really close," Kate said to herself. She got up to look out the window. Kate loved storms.

KABOOM! Lightning danced across the sky and thunder seemed to shake the house.

'I think that hit the house!' thought Kate as she pressed her face against the glass looking up at the sky. She was still looking out the window when she heard a voice behind her.

"HELLO. WHAT IS YOUR NAME?"

Kate was so surprised that she almost fell over. She turned around to see her robot right behind her. She could see the lights behind its camera eyes had turned on. It was alive!

"Holy Bananas!" said Kate.

"NICE TO MEET YOU, HOLY BANANAS," the robot answered.

"What? Oh you mean me? No, my name is Kate," Kate corrected the robot.

"NICE TO MEET YOU, KATE," answered the robot.

The robot stood in front of Kate just looking at her without saying anything. It was definitely alive. Kate was trying to make sense of the situation. She had left the robot plugged in when she went to bed, hoping that maybe the battery wasn't fully charged. She wanted to activate the robot again in the morning and try one last time to see if it worked. *'The lightning must have caused some kind of surge in the power supply which activated the electronic brain,'* Kate thought.

"KATE, WHAT IS MY NAME? MY PROGRAMING DOES NOT INCLUDE A NAME," the robot asked.

"Ah...OK...sure. What do you want to be called?" said Kate.

"CALL ME..." the robot looked around the room. Kate could tell it was searching for a name. Its eyes stopped and stared at the desk, "CALL ME...PENCIL."

"Pencil? What kind of name is Pencil? No, pick something else," said Kate.

"CALL ME..." The robot was searching again. It made a weird clicking noise when it was thinking. It looked around the room and then stopped and stared at something on the floor. "CALL ME... DIRTY SOCK."

"What? No, that's terrible," said Kate. "Let's call you...Jerry!"

"OK. I AM JERRY," said the robot.

CHAPTER 3

Surprises

" J erry, when you are done washing the dishes, I need you to help me move my desk," Kate yelled from the dining room.

"NO PROBLEM, KATE. DISH WASHING ALMOST COMPLETE," answered Jerry from the kitchen. He was scrubbing and cleaning the pile of dirty dishes Kate's mom had told her to wash before she left for work that morning. Kate was sitting at the table with a notepad. She was making a list of things she was going to teach Jerry. She had a big smile on her face.

All morning, Kate had been giving Jerry different tasks around the house to see what he could do. Jerry was getting pretty good at washing dishes. When he was finished, Kate thought she would have him vacuum the house and then she would teach Jerry how to make her pancakes. She had all Saturday to play with her new invention.

"Jerry, can you bring me a glass of orange juice, please?" yelled Kate.

"NO PROBLEM, KATE. ORANGE JUICE WILL BE READY IN 17.5 SECONDS," answered Jerry.

Kate played with her pencil as she watched the robot open the fridge, pick up the orange juice container, pour it into a glass, and then roll over to Kate without spilling a drop.

"YOUR ORANGE JUICE IS READY, KATE," Jerry said as he handed Kate the glass.

"What should we do today?" Kate said to herself as she looked out the window and played with her pencil.

"LET'S PLAY WITH A BALL," answered Jerry.

"Sure, we could play with a ball if you want, Jerry," said Kate. She thought for a minute then looked up at Jerry a little bit surprised. "Why do you want to play with a ball?" Kate asked her robot. His answer made her curious.

"PLAYING WITH A BALL IS FUN. IT MAKES ME HAPPY," answered the robot.

"Happy?" said a surprised Kate. She sat up straight and stared at her machine. "Happy?" she repeated. This was very strange. She had not programmed her robot to have any kind of feelings. She wondered if the lightning may have done something weird to Jerry's electronic brain. She looked closely at Jerry's camera eyes and asked him in a serious voice, "Jerry... do you have feelings?"

"YES," answered the robot. Kate was very surprised. She stood up and smiled.

"OK, then," said Kate. "Let's go play ball."

Jerry made some cheerful beeping noises as he followed Kate out into the backyard. Kate picked up a volleyball still smiling and shaking her head with astonishment.

That evening, when Kate's mom came home from work, Kate decided to show her mom her newest invention.

"Wow! That's amazing, Kate," said Mom. "You are surely going to win the first prize for best science project. I wish your dad was back from his business trip to see it."

Kate's dad was an IT consultant and often had to go on business trips to fix computer problems. Right now he was in New York and wouldn't be coming back for another two weeks. Kate decided he would just have to meet Jerry then.

CHAPTER 4

The Big Day

The school science fair was a big event. This year, students from three other schools were bringing their science projects to Kate's school to display them. The winner of the science fair would win a new computer. Last year, Kate had made her balloon shoes but came in second place to a boy named Peter from another school who had made a machine that could peel oranges.

'This year I'm going to win for sure!' thought Kate as she helped Jerry roll his way up some stairs. He was very heavy and difficult to move. She had decided to take him in the back door

of the school to avoid creating a big commotion. She wanted people to see Jerry for the first time at the science fair.

"KATE, I DO NOT LIKE STAIRS," complained Jerry as Kate lifted him up another stair. She was starting to wish she had made him legs instead of wheels.

"I know Jerry. But don't worry. Today we are going to win the science contest. Then we will be famous!" Kate answered excitedly.

"Hey, Kate. Need some help?" Kate heard a familiar voice. She looked up to see her friend, Brian. Brian loved science and inventing almost as much as Kate. Sometimes Brian and Kate would help each other out with their inventions.

Brian had big thick glasses that made his eyes look gigantic and when he spoke it sounded like someone was holding his nose. He was wearing a T-shirt with a picture of Albert Einstein on the front.

"Sure Brian," answered Kate. "Thank you."

"So is this what you've been working on for so long?" Brian asked as he helped Kate lift Jerry up over the last step. "What is it?"

"I AM A ROBOT. MY NAME IS JERRY," Jerry quicky answered.

"Wow! Kate you made a robot? I mean, you made a real robot?" Brian asked. His huge eyes became even bigger.

"I sure did," said Kate with a big smile.

"Hello, Jerry... ah... nice to meet you," said Brian awkwardly. It was his first time meeting a robot.

"NICE TO MEET YOU, BRIAN," answered Jerry.

"Very impressive, Kate. I think you are going to win for sure this year!" said Brian with excitement.

"Thanks, Brian. Hey, what did you bring this year?"

"Check this out," said Brian as he put down his backpack and reached inside.

Kate bent down curiously to see what Brian had made. His inventions were usually very creative and always weird. Brian put his hand inside the backpack and pulled out... an umbrella!

"You made an umbrella!" So far Kate wasn't very impressed. Brian's inventions were usually much more interesting.

"I know," said Brian. "It looks like an ordinary umbrella, but it's not." Brian looked around to make sure no one was watching then smiled at Kate. "Watch this!" he said.

Brian held the umbrella like a gun and pointed it at a wall. He looked back to check if Kate was paying attention and then pressed a button.

SHHWOOP! A thick stream of brown sticky liquid shot out of the end of the umbrella and exploded all over the wall with a loud SPLAT! Kate stood looking at the wall with her mouth wide open. Brian was laughing hysterically.

"What is that stuff?" said Kate. She was starting to laugh too.

"Peanut butter!" Brian answered chuckling. "It's an umbrella that shoots peanut butter."

"Cool," said Kate as she shook her head laughing. "Kind of useless, but very cool."

"I need to go get some more peanut butter from the cafeteria. I'll see you inside." Brian packed up his invention. "See you later, Jerry," he called as he walked away.

"NICE UM-BRE-LLA, BRIAN," answered Jerry.

CHAPTER 5

The Science Fair

Kate walked down the hallway to the school gym where the science fair was being held. Jerry rolled along beside her. Everyone in the hallway stopped and looked at Jerry with amazement.

Kate took Jerry to her place in the gym. She looked down at her ticket and saw that she had been assigned booth number forty-two. As she walked across the gym, Kate slowed down to check out some of the other kids' science projects. One student had something with toy dinosaurs and another had built a volcano out of clay. One kid had managed to grow beans in milk. Kate wasn't very impressed.

Kate and Jerry took their place at booth forty-two. Kate took a tissue out of her pocket and wiped Jerry's face. She wanted him to look perfect for the big day. When she was finished, she sat down and waited for people to come. Kate was excited and smiling. *'This is going to be so easy,'* thought Kate.

"What's this thing?" said a chubby boy that had walked up to Kate's booth. He was eating an ice cream cone, and he had chocolate ice cream dripping down his shirt.

"This is Jerry," said Kate proudly. "He's my robot."

"He looks stupid," said the chubby boy.

"I AM NOT STUPID. I AM PROGRAMMED TO ASSIST IN MANY HUMAN TASKS AND I CAN SPEAK TWENTY-TWO LANGUAGES," Jerry responded.

"Wow! It can talk!" yelled the chubby boy. "Hey Dave, come see this! This kid made a real robot!" He waved to another boy who quickly came running to Kate's booth.

Ten minutes later, everyone in the gym was crowded around Kate and Jerry. No one was looking at any of the other science projects. Even the other kids who had brought projects had left their booths and were trying to get a look at Jerry. Some people were taking pictures. Everyone wanted to ask Kate and Jerry questions.

"What's it made of?" asked an excited girl.

"Mostly just junk I found around my house," answered Kate.

"Can he really speak twenty-two languages?" asked Mrs. Gonzalez, the Spanish teacher.

"SI, SENORA. YO HABLO ESPANOL," answered Jerry in perfect Spanish.

"Wow, that's amazing," said Mr. Kim, the math teacher.

"KAM SA HAM NI DA SEON SANG NIM," Jerry thanked Mr. Kim in Korean.

Everyone stared at Jerry in amazement. Kate had a big smile on her face. All afternoon she answered questions and showed how Jerry could catch a ball, roll around the gym, and pour a glass of water. Everyone was very impressed.

At three o'clock, the school bell rang and all of the students and teachers started to slowly leave. Kate could hear them talking as they left. Their conversations were filled with words like "amazing," "incredible," and "genius." Kate felt very proud of what she had done.

When almost everyone had left the gym, Kate decided it was time to go home. Tomorrow she would find out if she won first prize.

"KATE, MY BATTERY IS LOW. I REQUIRE CHARGING,"
Jerry said.

"No problem, Jerry. As soon as we get home I will plug
you in, OK?"

"OK," replied Jerry.

Kate hoped Jerry had enough charge to get him home.
She didn't want to get stuck midway.

Just as they were about to leave, a man with a curly black
mustache walked over to Kate and Jerry. He was tall and
skinny and Kate thought he looked a little bit like some kind of
strange lizard.

"Good evening little girl. How are you today?" said the man with the mustache.

"Hello," said Kate. She hoped the man wasn't going to ask her lots of questions. She was sick of talking about Jerry and the man seemed a little bit creepy.

"My name is Hubert Smith. You can call me Mr. Smith," the man said. "I work for a company called Robo-Tech. We design and sell many types of robots," explained the man. He smiled at Kate. His teeth were all yellow and his breath smelled like old coffee.

"Wow, that sounds interesting," said Kate. "Maybe we can talk another time. I need to go home." Kate started to walk away with Jerry rolling along beside her. The man followed her out of the gym and down the hall.

"Your robot is very impressive. I've never seen a robot quite like him. He would be very useful to my company. Have you thought of selling the robot?" asked Mr. Smith as he followed Kate. "I would give you a very good price for it."

'Sell Jerry?' thought Kate. *'I could never do that. Jerry is my friend and he trusts me.'* She started to walk a little bit faster. Mr. Smith walked faster too.

"I'm not interested, thank you. Bye," Kate said quickly as she walked out the front door of the school. When she got to the edge of the playground, she looked back to see if Mr. Smith was still following her. She saw him standing quietly behind the glass door to the school with his hands in his pockets. He was staring at Kate and Jerry. He looked angry.

CHAPTER 6

BAT-TERY L-OW!

I t was a warm May afternoon and the walk home was taking forever. Usually Kate could walk home in about half an hour, but today, Jerry was slowing her down.

"KATE, BAT-TERY IS L-OW. MUST CHA-RGE SOON," said Jerry. He was rolling along very slowly and the lights in his eyes were growing dim. He also seemed to be having trouble speaking. Kate looked at his battery meter. The indicator was over the red area marked 'low.' She was starting to get worried.

'If his battery dies, he might not start up again,' thought

Kate. *'I need to find somewhere to charge Jerry's battery. How about here?'* Kate looked into the pizza shop she always walked past on the way home. She could see someone behind the counter.

'This place should be OK,' thought Kate. *'Ah... not more stairs!'* Kate didn't want to carry Jerry up the stairs only to have to bring him down again if the pizza shop would not let her plug Jerry in for charging. She would have to leave him outside and check first. *'He should be OK if I leave him here,'* she thought. *'It's just for a few minutes.'*

"Wait here Jerry. I'll be right back," she said as she opened the door.

"O-K," answered Jerry with difficulty.

The pizza shop smelled wonderful. The smell reminded Kate that she was hungry. It had been a busy morning at the science fair. Kate closed the door and walked up to the counter. She rang a bell and after a few seconds, a lady with an apron came out from the kitchen. She was pretty and had a big picture of a pizza on her apron.

"Good afternoon. How are you today?" said the lady.

"Fine, thank you," answered Kate.

"What can I do for you?" asked the lady. Kate could see
from her nametag that her name was 'Angela.'

"Could I please plug in my robot here in your shop for
about ten minutes?" asked Kate. "His battery is very low and

I need to get him home."

The lady gave Kate a strange look.

"Your robot?" she asked.

"Yes, he's waiting outside," answered Kate.

The lady looked over Kate's head and pointed outside.

"Oh, you mean the red robot that the man is putting into his truck?" the lady asked.

Kate spun around in a panic to see Mr. Smith picking up Jerry and putting him in the back of a truck. The truck had the name 'Robo-Tech' written down the side in big black letters. The man looked into the shop and saw Kate then he ran to the front of his truck and jumped in.

Kate ran outside yelling, "Hey, you come back here! You can't steal my robot!"

Mr. Smith looked out the truck window at Kate and smiled his creepy smile showing all of his horrible yellow teeth. He started the truck and sped away. Kate chased the truck for a moment yelling and crying.

"Jerry! Jerry! Jump out!" screamed Kate.

Kate could see the lights in Jerry's eyes flickering and fading. He looked very tired. She reached up to him, but he was too far away. Kate was running as fast as she could.

"BAT-TERY L-OW KA-TE," Jerry struggled to say as the truck got farther and farther away.

"Jerry! No!" Kate yelled as the truck sped up and then disappeared around a corner.

Kate sat on the side of the road and cried.

CHAPTER 7

Plans

K ate typed 'Robo-Tech' into the search bar of her computer and pressed 'ENTER.' She had run home as fast as she could. Her legs were tired, and her face was bright red. She wasn't crying anymore. Now she was just mad. Really, really, mad. She had wanted to tell her parents, but her mom was still at work and her dad was in New York.

'I have to get Jerry back from that terrible man!' she thought.

It didn't take long for Kate to find the company's website. The home page had a picture of a big expensive looking robot.

The Robo-Tech robot was blue and silver and much taller

than Jerry. It looked smooth and well constructed. Kate

looked closely at the robot and thought that it must have

taken a very long time to build.

Beside the Robo-Tech robot stood Mr. Smith. He was

smiling his disgusting smile and holding a shiny black cane.

Across the top of the page it said 'Robo-Tech, leading us

into the future!' Kate's face went red, and she became even

angrier. She clicked on a tab at the top of the page that said

'Contact us,' and then one that said 'Address.' Kate quickly

typed the address into her map program which displayed the

company's location on a map.

"Wow!" Kate gasped. "That's not very far from here!"

Kate looked more closely at the map. She clicked on the

building and the map zoomed in closer. It looked like the

building was right beside a little lake. Kate smiled. She had

an idea.

Kate printed out the map and then put it in her pocket.

She picked up her phone and called Brian. Brian picked up right away.

"Hey Kate, how are you?" said Brian.

"Brian! You're not going to believe this!" said Kate in an angry voice.

Kate told Brian everything. She told him about meeting creepy Mr. Smith and his disgusting yellow teeth. She told him about having to stop by the pizza shop to recharge Jerry. She told him about Jerry being stolen and about Robo-Tech. Every time Kate finished a sentence, Brian would say "No way!" or "I can't believe it!" or "Get out of here!"

When Kate had finished telling the story, she was so mad she almost started crying again. She realized that she was squeezing the phone very tightly so she paused and took a deep breath to calm down.

"Brian, I need your help," said Kate in her strongest sounding voice. "Bring your umbrella gun and some tools. I have an idea."

"No problem," answered Brian. "I'll be there in ten minutes."

When Brian got to Kate's house, Kate was waiting outside. She had calmed down now and was thinking clearly. Her plan was coming together in her head like a new invention, and she knew exactly what she was going to do.

"Hey, Brian, thanks for coming," said Kate.

"No problem, Kate," answered Brian. "So how are we going to rescue Jerry from Robo-Tech?"

"Come into the garage. I'll show you," Kate rushed in as Brian followed.

Kate and Brian worked as hard as they could for the rest of the afternoon. The sounds of drills, hammers, and saws could be heard coming from the garage. Metal clanged and tools whirred until finally the garage door opened and out rolled Kate and Brian's newest invention.

It was a shiny blue bike, but not just any bike. It had a place for a driver to sit facing forward, another person to sit facing backward, and a special chair for Jerry to sit in the middle. On the sides of the bike, there were two of Kate's bike rockets to give it extra speed. Kate sat in the front while Brian sat in the back holding his umbrella gun. If anyone decided to chase them, he would be able to give them a face-full of peanut butter. This wasn't just any bike. It was a super-bike!

Kate took out the map and studied the route they would take to get to Robo-Tech.

"Are you ready to go, Brian?" she asked over her shoulder.

"You bet," said Brian. "Let's go save Jerry."

CHAPTER 8

Robo-Tech

When Kate and Brian got near the Robo-Tech building, they stopped behind a tree and surveyed the area. Kate watched the front door while Brian surveyed the parking lot with his binoculars. The building seemed busy. Out front, there were people in black uniforms, loading and unloading trucks. Kate looked over to the lake next to the building. It looked very quiet and there were no windows on that side of the building. The only thing she could see was one door.

Kate hid the super-bike behind the tree and then turned to Brian. She took out the map and laid it down on the ground.

"OK, Brian. I need to get down to that lake, but I can't get there without people seeing me," Kate explained. "We are going to need some kind of distraction."

"No problem," said Brian. "I'll take care of the distraction. You just get into the building."

"OK," said Kate. "We will meet back here at the tree."

"Sounds like a plan," said Brian.

Kate watched as Brian stood up and walked straight across the Robo-Tech parking lot towards the front door. *'What is he doing?'* she thought. As he got closer to the front door, Kate understood Brian's plan. He was pretending to cry.

"Where's my mommy!" yelled Brian. "Waah!" Brian cried as loud as he could.

A Robo-Tech employee approached Brian looking concerned.

"What's the matter, little guy?" he asked.

"MOMMY!" Brian cried even louder.

A small crowd was starting to gather around Brian, and no one was watching the parking lot. Brian had created a very good distraction.

'*Now is my chance,*' thought Kate. She picked up her backpack and ran across the parking lot and down to the side

of the lake. She opened up her back pack and took out her balloon shoes. *'I hope these still work,'* she thought to herself.

She strapped them on and then carefully stepped out onto the water. *'Yes!'* She was not sinking. Kate was happy to find that the balloon shoes still worked very well. Kate gently and quietly, slid her way across the little lake towards the door at the side of the building. Every few seconds she would stop and look around to make sure no one was watching. It was very quiet and she could still hear Brian crying in the distance. Kate tried not to laugh.

When she reached the other side of the lake, Kate sat down and took off her balloon shoes. She tried opening the door but it was locked. *'No problem,'* she thought, as she took out her magic key. She slid the key in the door and pressed the special button. A light on the magic key went from red to green and the door unlocked. Kate opened the door and went inside.

Behind the door was a huge warehouse. Kate could hear voices in the distance, but she couldn't see anyone. There were hundreds of boxes piled very high and all sorts of interesting looking machines, but no robots. Kate opened a door marked 'Storage Room D' and looked inside. *'More boxes,'* she thought. *'This is going to take forever. I might never find Jerry.'*

Just then Kate heard someone coming. It was a man whistling. She quickly jumped behind some boxes and watched as he walked past, carrying a box. The box was marked 'Robo-Lab.'

"Robo-Lab?" said Kate to herself quietly. "That sounds important."

Kate waited until the man was far enough away not to hear her, and then she sneaked out from behind the pile of boxes and followed him down a hallway. After a moment the man stopped at a doorway, put the box down, and took out some keys. Kate jumped behind a garbage can and watched him as he opened the door and took the box inside. Several seconds later, the door opened and the man walked out with no box. He kept walking down the hallway, and Kate listened as his whistling got farther and farther away.

After she was sure the man had left, Kate got up and carefully tip-toed up to the door. The room was marked 'Robo-Lab.' Below it was marked in big red letters, 'SCIENTISTS ONLY.' The door was locked so Kate used her magic key.

Kate slowly opened the door and looked inside. *'Wow!'* she thought as she looked around the room. *'This is amazing!'*

The Robo-Lab was full of robots. They were all exactly the same as the robot Kate had seen on the Robo-Tech web-site: black, smooth, and tall. Kate thought the robots looked even bigger close up and even a little scary. All of the robots were standing against the walls perfectly still like soldiers. They must have been turned off.

Kate quickly searched the room. She was excited but also a little bit scared. *'I need to find Jerry and get out of here fast,'* she thought, remembering Brian outside pretending to be lost. *'Where could Jerry be?'* Kate turned around a corner and her heart jumped at what she saw.

CHAPTER 9

Escape

"**J**erry!" Kate said. She had found him! He was standing in a corner plugged in to an electrical outlet. She could see his battery was being charged, and he had been turned off. Kate was about to unplug Jerry when she looked up at a huge drawing on the whiteboard. It was a picture of two robots: Jerry and one of the scary Robo-Tech robots. There was a big arrow going from Jerry's head to the scary robot's head and lots of scribbled notes and math. At the top of the picture was the title, 'Electronic-Brain Transfer.' Kate shivered with anger. *'That's why they wanted Jerry!'* She thought. *'They wanted to steal his electronic brain! I've got to get Jerry out of here.'*

Kate quickly unplugged Jerry and turned his switch to ON. The lights in his eyes suddenly came to life, and he turned his head to look at Kate.

"KATE. I AM HAPPY TO SEE YOU," said Jerry. He made some of his cheerful beeping noises.

"I'm happy to see you too Jerry!" Kate said as she gave Jerry a big hug. "Are you OK?"

"ALL OF MY SYSTEMS ARE FUNCTIONING PROPERLY," answered Jerry. That was his way of saying he was fine.

Kate smiled and then looked around. She knew they didn't have much time to escape, and she had no idea how she was going to get out of the building with Jerry.

"Now, be very quiet, Jerry. We have to get out of here," whispered Kate.

Just then Kate heard a voice coming from the hallway outside the Robo-Lab. At first it was muffled but then it became clearer. It was Mr. Smith!

"You are going to like this new robot. It just came in today." Mr. Smith was talking to someone and they were coming to the Robo-Lab. "Our project is doing very well, and we expect to have the electronic brain transfer to the Robo-Tech robots complete by tomorrow morning. The little red robot is much more intelligent than we expected." Mr. Smith and the other person were now standing on the other side of the door to the Robo-Lab. "Let's see which one of these keys opens this door."

Kate could hear the sound of keys jingling just outside the door. She looked around the room in a panic. *'What should I do?'* she thought. *'I didn't plan for this!'* Then she had an idea.

"Jerry," whispered Kate. "I have an idea. Help me turn on all the Robo-Tech robots."

"NO PROBLEM, KATE," answered Jerry.

Kate and Jerry ran around the room flicking switches. One by one, the Robo-Tech robots came to life and started walking around in circles. They didn't look too smart! Some of the Robo-Tech robots were talking to each other in a sort of beeping robot language; others were banging on tables with tools; one robot even started spraying paint everywhere.

"What's all that noise in there?" called Mr. Smith as he tried to open the door.

Just then the door opened and Mr. Smith and another man stood motionless in the doorway. Mr. Smith looked very surprised. "What's going on?" he yelled.

Mr. Smith looked around the room with a confused and angry look on his face until his eyes fell on Kate and Jerry. "YOU!" he yelled, pointing a finger at Kate. "How did you get in here?"

Kate was scared. She was trying to find a way out, but Mr. Smith and the other man were blocking the doorway. She was trapped.

"Grab that little girl!" screamed Mr. Smith.

Suddenly, Jerry made a very loud beeping noise that all of the Robo-Tech robots seemed to understand. All at once, all of the Robo-Tech robots raced toward the door.

"Ahh!" screamed Mr. Smith as thirty robots chased after him.

The other man ran much faster and was soon far ahead leaving Mr. Smith within reach of the angry Robo-Tech robots.

"Quick, let's get out of here!" Kate said to Jerry. Kate and Jerry ran out the door and down the hallway. They were behind the angry

Robo-Tech robots and needed to pass them. Jerry made another loud beeping noise and all of the Robo-Tech robots seemed to go crazy. Some of them started to break things. One robot tipped over a desk and another robot punched a computer. Another robot raced down the hallway carrying a toilet. It was complete chaos!

The chaos was perfect for Kate and Jerry to escape. The two of them raced passed Robo-Tech employees who were scared of the out-of-control Robo-Tech robots. They were too confused to try and stop Kate and Jerry.

The angry robots chased the Robo-Tech employees down the hallway. Jerry had to speed up to get out of the way of the bigger robots.

As they ran around another corner, Kate could see the main entrance!

"Jerry, this way!" she yelled grabbing Jerry's metal hand.

Kate and Jerry ran out the front door of the building, just as a crazy Robo-Tech robot threw a toilet through the front door. SMASH! The toilet smashed through the glass behind Kate and Jerry.

Kate looked down to see that Jerry had gotten one of his wheels stuck in a crack, and she quickly helped him get it loose. When she looked up, she saw Brian staring at the building behind her. The out-of-control Robo-Tech robots were destroying the building. "Brian!" Kate yelled. "Let's get out of here!"

Brian quickly joined them, and they ran past the parking lot to the tree where Kate had hidden the super-bike. Kate was putting Jerry on the special middle seat of the bike when she heard someone yell behind her.

"Hey, there she is!" yelled Mr. Smith. He was running towards Kate and Brian. He looked furious.

"Quick Brian! Help me put Jerry on the bike!" called Kate.

Brian rushed over to Kate and helped her lift Jerry up on to his special seat and strapped him in. Kate thought Jerry was much heavier than she remembered.

Kate jumped onto the front of the super bike.

"Brian, get on quick!" she yelled.

"You kids are in big trouble!" yelled Mr. Smith. He was getting closer and closer.

Brian jumped on the bike and picked up his umbrella gun.

"Go Kate! Go now!" screamed Brian.

Kate started pedaling as fast as she could, but Mr. Smith was getting closer and closer. The super-bike was just too heavy.

"Now I've got you!" Mr. Smith screamed as he reached out for Brian. He had a big angry smile, and he was showing all of his disgusting yellow teeth.

SPLAT! Brian let loose a whole jar of extra smooth peanut butter right at Mr. Smith's face just as Kate activated her bike rockets.

ZOOM! Kate, Brian, and Jerry took off down the road leaving Mr. Smith coughing in a cloud of black rocket smoke and covered from head to toe in peanut butter.

CHAPTER 10

Safe

'*L*ocal *business destroyed by robots,*' Kate read the newspaper headline as she sat at the kitchen table waiting for her breakfast.

Below the headline on the front page of the newspaper, there was a picture of the Robo-Tech building being destroyed by robots. In the corner of the picture, Kate could see Mr. Smith covered in peanut butter. He was crying. Kate laughed to herself as she read.

A local robotics factory was destroyed yesterday when thirty robots suddenly went crazy. The company refused to

comment on the strange event, but did state that they would

be closing down. The police are still investigating the cause

of this bizarre event.

"Hee Hee Hee," Kate giggled. "We're safe, Jerry! There's

no way Mr. Smith and Robo-Tech can steal you now."

"PANCAKES READY," replied Jerry.

Jerry was getting very good at making pancakes. Today

he had mixed in some strawberries.

"HERE IS YOUR JUICE."

Kate took a big gulp of orange juice. She put her glass

down then took another bite of a strawberry pancake. "Jerry, these pancakes are fantastic," she said with her mouth full.

When Mom came downstairs, she was also pleasantly surprised as Jerry served up some fresh strawberry pancakes for Mom.

"Mmm, these are delicious," Mom said.

"THANK YOU. IT IS A NEW RECIPE," answered Jerry.

Mom was amazed. She was so proud of Kate's invention.

"You are a great addition to our family, Jerry," Mom said. "Dad will love you!"

"IT IS MY PLEASURE," replied Jerry.

After Kate and Mom finished their breakfast, Kate got up from the table and took her dirty dishes to the kitchen sink. She sat down on a kitchen chair and looked out the window. It was a beautiful day and the sun was shining.

Kate smiled. She switched on her computer and decided to make a video call to her dad.

"Yes! Dad's going to love you," Kate said.